BARNYARD SONG

by **Rhonda Gowler Greene**   illustrated by **Robert Bender**

ATHENEUM BOOKS FOR YOUNG READERS

Atheneum Books for Young Readers
An imprint of Simon & Schuster
Children's Publishing Division
1230 Avenue of the Americas
New York, New York 10020

Book design by Michael Nelson
The text of this book is set in Versailles Bold.
The illustrations are rendered in animator's paint
   on acetate backed with black paper.

First Edition
Printed in Hong Kong by South China Printing Co. (1988) Ltd.
10 9 8 7 6 5 4

Library of Congress Cataloging-in-Publication Data
Greene, Rhonda Gowler.
Barnyard song / by Rhonda Gowler Greene ;
illustrated by Robert Bender.—1st ed.
p.   cm.
Summary: When the barnyard animals
catch the flu, the farmer takes care of
them until their usual voices return.
ISBN 0-689-80758-9
[1. Domestic animals—Fiction.
2. Animal sounds—Fiction.
3. Sick—Fiction. 4. Stories in
rhyme.]
I. Bender, Robert, ill.
II. Title.
PZ8.3.G824Bar 1997
[E]—dc20
96-1923

For Mom and in memory of Dad
—R. G. G.

For all the beasts that go A-H-H-H-CHOO! in our family:
Christina, Karen, Briana, Charmaine, Craig, Lawrence,
Teresa, Aaron, Rosemary, and Jim
—R. B.

On the farm on the hill on a blustery day,
Farmer was a-humming and storing heaps of hay.
The animals were singing all their usual notes
in their usual voices, in their usual throats . . .

Buzz, buzz
Mew, mew
Cock-a-doodle-doo

Oink, oink
Baa, baa
Moo, moo, moo

Here a **bray**.
There a **bray**.
Everywhere a **bray**.

Gobble, gobble
Quack, quack
Neigh, neigh, neigh . . .

when all of a sudden came a whisper of a sneeze,
the sneeze of Bee buzzing on the autumn breeze.
Well, that sneeze spun round and it wasn't very long
before the barnyard choir stopped singing their song.

No **buzz**.
No **mew**.
No **cock-a-doodle-doo**.
No **oink**.
No **baa**.
No **moo, moo, moo**.

No here a **bray**,
there a **bray**,
everywhere a **bray**.
No **gobble**, **gobble**,
quack, **quack**,
neigh, **neigh**, **neigh**.

Farmer called the doctor, and the nurse came too, and the three did agree it was the barnyard flu.

So for one long week all were put to bed
and the barnyard sounds went like this instead:

Buzz, 'CHOO!
Mew, SNIFF!
Cock-a-SQUAWK!-le-doo

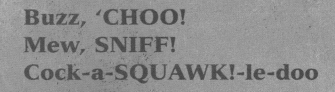

Oink, SQUEAL!
Baa, SNORT!
Moo, A-H-H-H-H-CHOO!

Here a **SNIFF!-LE.**
There a **SNUFF!-LE.**
Everywhere a **SNEEZE! ('CHOO!)**

Gobble, SCREECH!
Quack, HONK!
WHEEZE! WHEEZE! WHEEZE!

Well, Farmer cooked up kettles of savory soup

and served it by the bowlful to the barnyard group—

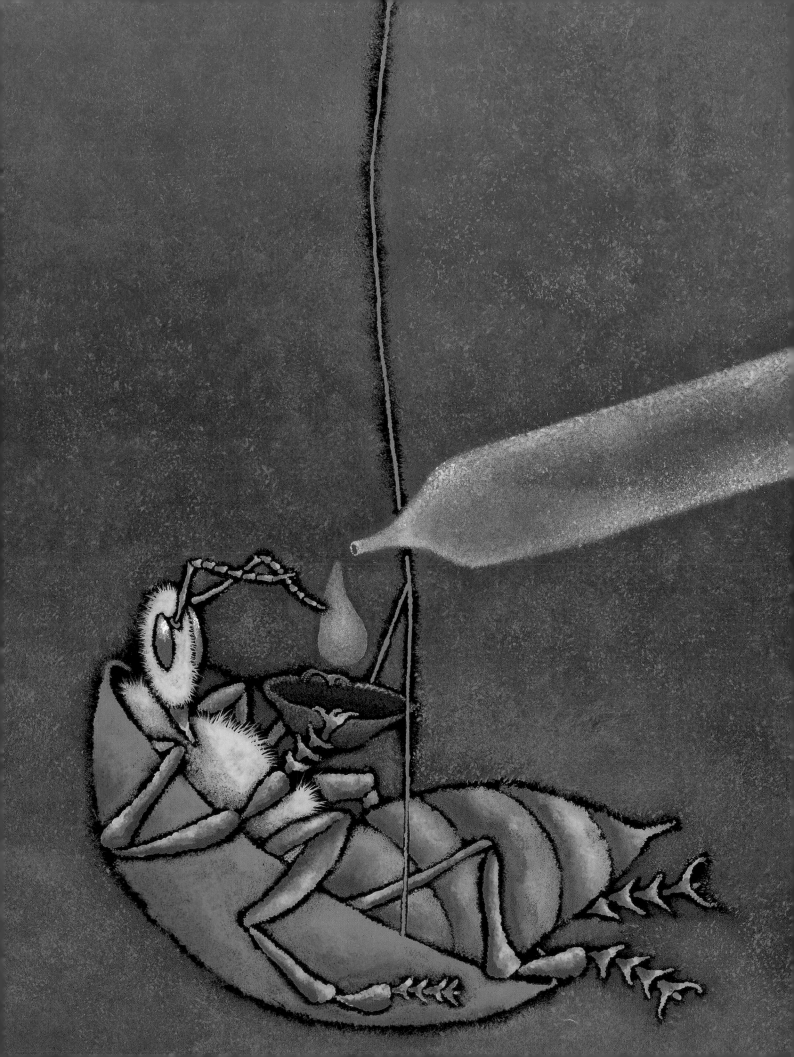

from the teeny, tiny bee who started it all

to the great big horse in the big, brown stall.

Then early one morning came a happy, humming sound.
"**Buzz, buzz**," buzzed Bee, flying round and round.

Soon all the others gathered with their usual throats
and out came the richest, sweetest barnyard notes!

Now Bee does "**Buzz**" and Cat says, "**Mew.**"
Rooster crows with a "**Cock-a-doodle-doo.**"
Pig says, "**Oink.**" All the piglets join in.
Sheep says, "**Baa.**" Let the song begin!

BUZZ, BUZZ
MEW, MEW
COCK-A-DOODLE-DOO

OINK, OINK
BAA, BAA
MOO, MOO, MOO

HERE A **BRAY**.
THERE A **BRAY**.
EVERYWHERE A **BRAY**.

GOBBLE, GOBBLE
QUACK, QUACK
NEIGH, NEIGH, NEIGH.

Now barnyard song gets sung all day
till the circle of sun sinks far away.
Animals bed down, sigh and yawn,
rest for tomorrow . . .

to sing again at dawn!

COCK-A-SQUAWK!-LE-DOO

BUZZ, 'CHOO!

WHEEZE! WHEEZE! WHEEZE!

QUACK, HONK!

GOBBLE, SCREECH!

SNIFFI-LE SNUFFI-LE SNEEZE!